THE ZIZ
AND THE
HANUKKAH
MIRACLE

by Jacqueline Jules
illustrated by Katherine Janus Kahn

KAR-BEN
PUBLISHING

To Alan, thank you for sharing your life with me. —J.J.

For Robert, thank you for a pair of eyes I can always trust. —K.J.K.

Text copyright © 2006 by Jacqueline Jules
Illustrations copyright © 2006 by Katherine Janus Kahn

Kar-Ben Publishing, Inc.
A division of Lerner Publishing Group
241 First Avenue North
Minneapolis, MN 55401 U.S.A.
1-800-4KARBEN

Website address: www.karben.com

Library of Congress Cataloging-in-Publication Data

Jules, Jacqueline, 1956–
    The Ziz and the Hanukkah miracle / by Jacqueline Jules ; illustrations by Katherine Janus Kahn.
        p.   cm.
    Summary: The Ziz, a huge and clumsy bird, helps the Maccabees find enough oil to light the
menorah and restore the temple, leading to the miracle that is celebrated every year at Hanukkah.
    ISBN-13: 978–1–58013–160–5 (lib. bdg. : alk. paper)
    ISBN-10: 1–58013–160–3 (lib. bdg. : alk. paper)
    [1. Animals, Mythical—Fiction. 2. Hanukkah—Fiction. 3. Jews—History—
586 B.C.–70 A.D.—Fiction.] I. Kahn, Katherine, ill. II. Title.
    PZ7.J92947Ziz 2006
    [E]—dc22   2005020910

Manufactured in the United States of America
1 – DP – 5/16/11

SINCE the beginning of time, animals have felt sad at summer's end, when night comes earlier and earlier each day.

No one was sadder than the Ziz, a gigantic yellow bird with huge red wings and a purple-feathered forehead, who lived on top of a mountain.

When the days were short, the Ziz didn't feel sleepy at sunset. Even worse, the Ziz couldn't see to make his dinner. He couldn't tell if he was picking up a cucumber or an ear of corn.

"Yuck!" the Ziz grumbled, "I hate cucumbers!"

The Ziz decided he needed light in
the evenings. But where could he get it?
"I know!" the Ziz flapped his wings
and danced. He loved coming up with
good ideas. "I'll get some fireflies."

The Ziz flew to a warm wet place and chased fireflies with a net.

But when he got them back to his nest, they wouldn't glow.
"What's wrong?" cried the Ziz.

"We don't like being squished together in this net," the fireflies said. "Let us out and we'll share our lights."

"That sounds fair," the Ziz said. He opened the net, and all the fireflies flew away.

"Wait!" the Ziz called.

The fireflies were gone. He needed another idea.

"I know!" the Ziz said. "I'll get some lantern fish! They can't fly away."

The next night, he stood in the ocean. The Ziz was so huge, the water only came up to his knees. As soon as he saw the bright lights of the lantern fish, he scooped them up into a pot.

"Give me light!" the Ziz commanded.

"No!" the lantern fish said. "We don't like it in here!"

The Ziz begged for hours, but the fish refused to share their lights. He needed another idea.

A full moon peeked out from under the clouds
and then disappeared.

"That's it!" the Ziz flapped his wings. "I'll catch
the moon!"

He flew up into the sky with a huge piece of rope
and tugged and tugged. The Ziz was the biggest
bird on earth, but he couldn't budge the moon.

"What am I going to do?" The Ziz
plopped back down in his nest, discouraged.
He had done everything he could on his
own. It was time to ask God for help.

The next day, the Ziz
flew to Mount Sinai, the
special place where he
always talked with God.

"I can't see to eat my dinner!"
the Ziz complained.

"You're right." God's big voice rumbled through the clouds.
"The days are short this time of year."

"Will you fix it?"

"No," God said firmly. "But I can make it easier to bear."

A bolt of lightning hit the ground. The Ziz turned around to
see a lamp filled with oil.

"What's this?" the Ziz asked.

"Take it home," God commanded. "And see."

Every evening, the oil lamp burned brightly. The Ziz could see to eat his dinner and fluff up the bed in his nest. He could even read himself a bedtime scroll.

Light! Light! A flicker, flame, or spark.
Makes my heart happy in the dark.

The Ziz watched the lovely flame for hours, singing and smiling. But he wasn't the only one. Raccoons, foxes, hedgehogs, rabbits, owls, and other little animals crept closer and closer each night. They needed something to brighten up the long dark hours too. One night, the Ziz saw fifty pairs of eyes enjoying his beautiful lamp!

"NO!" the Ziz squawked. "It's mine! It's mine!"

The Ziz was so upset, he couldn't sleep. In the morning, he grabbed his light and took off to find another place to live.

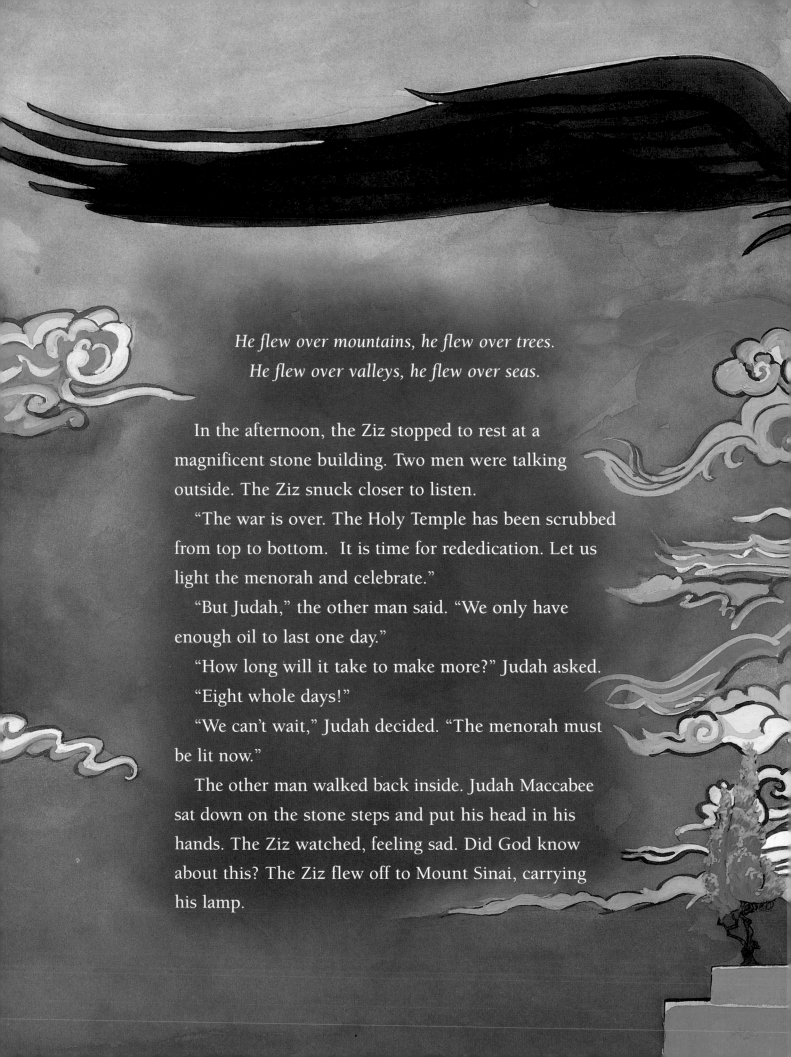

He flew over mountains, he flew over trees.
He flew over valleys, he flew over seas.

In the afternoon, the Ziz stopped to rest at a magnificent stone building. Two men were talking outside. The Ziz snuck closer to listen.

"The war is over. The Holy Temple has been scrubbed from top to bottom. It is time for rededication. Let us light the menorah and celebrate."

"But Judah," the other man said. "We only have enough oil to last one day."

"How long will it take to make more?" Judah asked.

"Eight whole days!"

"We can't wait," Judah decided. "The menorah must be lit now."

The other man walked back inside. Judah Maccabee sat down on the stone steps and put his head in his hands. The Ziz watched, feeling sad. Did God know about this? The Ziz flew off to Mount Sinai, carrying his lamp.

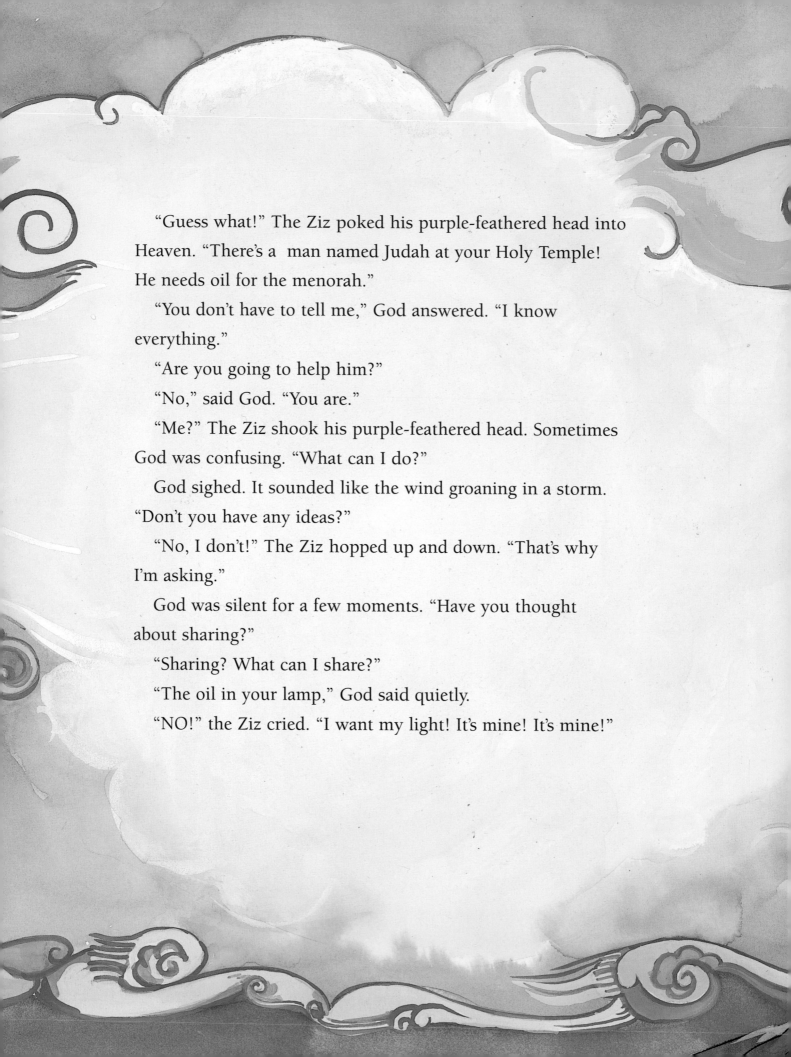

"Guess what!" The Ziz poked his purple-feathered head into Heaven. "There's a man named Judah at your Holy Temple! He needs oil for the menorah."

"You don't have to tell me," God answered. "I know everything."

"Are you going to help him?"

"No," said God. "You are."

"Me?" The Ziz shook his purple-feathered head. Sometimes God was confusing. "What can I do?"

God sighed. It sounded like the wind groaning in a storm. "Don't you have any ideas?"

"No, I don't!" The Ziz hopped up and down. "That's why I'm asking."

God was silent for a few moments. "Have you thought about sharing?"

"Sharing? What can I share?"

"The oil in your lamp," God said quietly.

"NO!" the Ziz cried. "I want my light! It's mine! It's mine!"

The Ziz flew away from Mount Sinai, without saying good-bye. He had never disobeyed God before. But God had never asked him to do anything this hard.

"Mine!" the Ziz sobbed. "Mine!"

The Ziz was crying so much, he couldn't see in the dark. He was headed straight for the Holy Temple, about to crash into the ceiling!

But just at the last second, the Ziz saw the seven-branched menorah shining through the open door.

"Whoops!" He swerved and hit the Temple steps instead.

The Ziz tiptoed up to the front door. He watched the light dancing on the Temple walls and ceiling.

"Pretty!" he cooed.

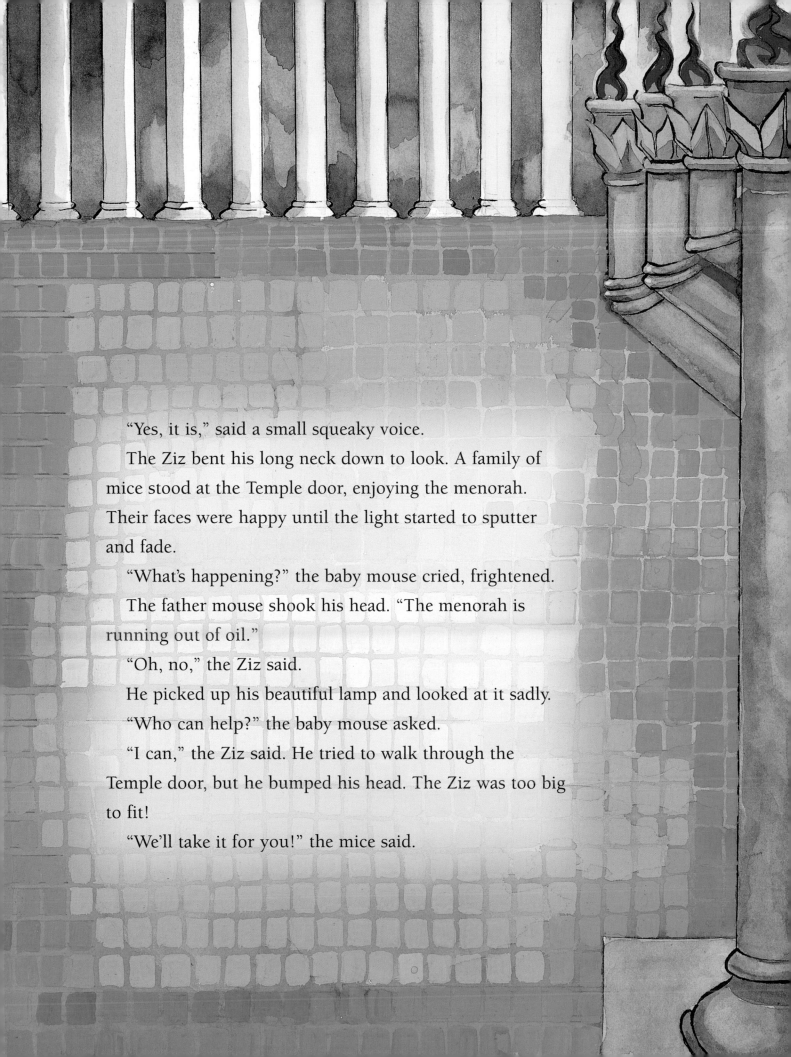

"Yes, it is," said a small squeaky voice.

The Ziz bent his long neck down to look. A family of mice stood at the Temple door, enjoying the menorah. Their faces were happy until the light started to sputter and fade.

"What's happening?" the baby mouse cried, frightened.

The father mouse shook his head. "The menorah is running out of oil."

"Oh, no," the Ziz said.

He picked up his beautiful lamp and looked at it sadly.

"Who can help?" the baby mouse asked.

"I can," the Ziz said. He tried to walk through the Temple door, but he bumped his head. The Ziz was too big to fit!

"We'll take it for you!" the mice said.

Together, the mouse family dragged the oil lamp up to the menorah. An owl flew in and helped them. Soon the light was burning as brightly as before. The Ziz jumped up and down, flapping his wings.

"It's beautiful! The most beautiful light ever!"

For eight nights, the mouse family helped the Ziz share his oil with the Maccabees.

On the ninth day, Judah rushed up the Temple steps with a jar of oil.

"It's a miracle! The light is still burning."

The Ziz picked up his lamp and flew back to his nest.

All day, he moped on his mountaintop. What would he do when it got dark? There was only a little bit of oil left in his lamp.

But at sunset, the Ziz had a surprise. His lamp was brighter than ever. The Ziz could see to make his dinner. He could fluff his bed and read his scrolls. Everything was just as it had been before. Except....

That night when the hedgehog, the fox, the raccoon, and all the little animals tiptoed up to his home, the Ziz invited them in. Together, they watched the lovely flame dancing in the darkness.

Light! Light! A flicker, flame, or spark.
Makes my heart happy in the dark.

Author's Note:
The holiday of Hanukkah commemorates the victory of the Maccabees over the Syrians more than two thousand years ago. After the war, the Maccabees scrubbed the Temple in Jerusalem for rededication. However, they only found one jar of pure oil — enough to last one day — to light the seven-branched candelabrum called the menorah. It took eight days to process more purified oil. A miracle occurred, and the menorah burned brightly for eight days. This is why Hanukkah is celebrated for eight days with the lighting of candles. The story never gives any explanation for the miracle of the oil. For all we know, the Ziz might have helped.